TALES FROM
THE LONDONSPHERE

NORA H. TAYLOR

ISBN 978-1-6671-6129-7

Illustrations by the author

Cover & title typeface: Pirate Vintage by Jumbo Designs

Author's Note

Ever since I was in first grade, I watched the eighth graders with awe. They were so grown up! And one of the things I admired the most was how they each did an amazing project and presented it at the end of the year. I would brainstorm about what my project would be and imagine how proud I would be when I had accomplished it!

This book has been an amazing experience to write, and throughout this entire process I have learned, explored, and grown as a writer. Ever since I was little, I have written stories—and now, to be able to hold this bound book that is full of my words and my ideas is simply wonderful.

This collection of short stories takes place in a world that has been in my imagination for a very long time, and it is awesome to finally have it down on paper.

So, thank you so much to everyone who has helped to make this happen, and I hope that reading this brings you as much joy as it brought to me while I was writing it.

PROLOGUE

Only the most unsavory characters choose to stop here on their way to brighter galaxies.

Only the most desperate souls seek work here, cleaning for a mad inventor perhaps, or cooking for an airship captain.

Despite its despicable nature, the planet itself is large, with a healthy atmosphere (*all the coal smoke and other filth is funneled through the planet's Greater Chimneys and released into space*) and a wonderful skyscape (*the planet is situated right next to Nebula Atmos, a glowing mass of emerald green, purple, and orange, that gives off wonderful solar flares each evening*). The Aether, the magical layer that runs through the very substance of everything, is strong on this planet. Warlocks tap into the Aether to power strange and diabolical contraptions. Coglings manipulate the Aether to create wrinkles in reality that they use for their own purposes. The Dualworld Society is obsessed with the idea that the Dual can be accessed through a hole in the Aether, and those with Shadowsight can see through the Aether into the Dual.

This planet is known as the Londonsphere.

Danger Wanted

The theatre in the East Sector is situated between a seedy pub and a metalworks factory.

The theatre itself is a tall, slightly tilted building, crumbling at the edges, with a large board nailed over the door proclaiming it

Moira and Grace's Theatric Co.

Tickets for sale.

Positively no credit.

The door was slightly ajar, and the strains of music from a bronze band could be heard playing the popular refrain, "My Love Is An Airship Captain." Inside, an assortment of patrons sat on dusty velvet seats and watched a troupe of performers in costume whirling about on the stage in time to the music. Dust motes danced in the beam of the spotlight, and the air smelled of oil, sweat, and that dusty scent that always hovers about old buildings.

Suddenly, the spotlight went out. There were thumps and muffled yelps as the performers rushed backstage to hide. A powerful searchlight swept through the grimy windows. There were shouts and gruff-called commands. The audience scattered, hiding under seats, melting into shadows, clinging to the ceiling. The door was kicked open, and automatons in red uniforms burst in, clicking and whirring as their ocular sensors scanned the room.

A dancer stumbled onto the stage, her eyes widening as she noticed the automatons. She was a large marmoset with golden fur, and her tail was encased in a mechanical brace made so that she could lift twice her body weight with it. She shrieked and made for the stage entrance, but one automaton shot a weighted net from a gun and pounced on the marmoset as she struggled to untangle herself. The automaton lugged its screeching, writhing parcel across the room and out the door. The other constable droids retreated and closed the door softly. The Constabulary Ship rose into the air.

The lights came back on. The theatre patrons stumbled, slithered, and flitted out of hiding, and settled back into their seats. The other dancers creeped back onstage and resumed their dance, though without the same fervor. The bronze band picked up the tune, and everything returned to as before.

However, when it came to the finale, the other dancers struggled to create their pyramid because they lacked the support of an enhanced tail. Up in the light booth, Grace sighed. She made a soft ululating call, and a dark lump that hung from a beam unfurled its furry wings and dropped onto Grace's head.

"Moira," Grace said, "go put up the *Dancer Wanted* poster again. It seems Sylph will not be in our employ anymore." The red panda nodded and flapped off to post a new notice on the front window.

Meanwhile, inside a dark prison cell, a thick bronze door shut and locked. The struggling net that was hurled inside unrolled to reveal a large marmoset in a tattered, sparkly costume curled up into a resigned ball. The marmoset sighed.

A week later, a Scavenger cat crawled over the piles of metal and bodies on a small moon orbiting the Londonsphere's Motherworld. She tugged at a filthy golden tail to pry off the mechanical brace.

That is how things are in the Londonsphere. For every death, one life is sustained.

THE SCAVENGER

The entire moon of Scrap was riddled with them. The braver souls born into poverty.

They stowed away to the moon on outgoing Dumpships, digging through the sea of the Motherworld's waste for things to sell, parts with which to build things, and anything usable to make their lives that much easier. Like Twitch.

Twitch was a Scavenger. She was a small brown cat, wearing a leather tunic with a hood, and aviation goggles, the typical garb of a Scavenger. She yawned as watery light filtered through a hole in her ragged, dull green tent. She crawled to the entrance and peered out. As far as she could see, the sea of Scrap met her eyes. Heaps of metal, piles of mechanics, and mounds of bodies. Twitch grabbed an empty sack and crept out of her tent. She slid down the pile of metal and landed on her Cycler.

The Cycler had been one of her most lucky discoveries. It was powered by Hovercraft technology and was shaped a bit like a scooter with a sidecar to store her finds. Twitch hopped onto the Cycler, clutching the handlebars with her front paws. She squeezed the throttle and shot off across the mountains of Scrap.

It was late in the afternoon, and the rays of the Greater Star Plato beat down through The Lesser Moon's thin atmosphere. Twitch tugged at the filthy tail of a dead marmoset, finally dislodging what looked like a mechanical tail brace. This was a good find. It would be a perfect gift for her sister, Jadyn. Twitch stuffed the brace into her sack. The sack was full, which meant it was time to get to the Dumpship landing zone before its next touchdown.

Twitch revved the engine of the Cycler and sped off over the waste fields. The heat was intensifying, and Twitch rode fast over the mountains of rubbish, her leather hood shading her head from the worst of the radioactive light. She was sweating under her fur.

At last, after a couple of grueling hours, Twitch pulled her Cycler to a stop a few piles from the Dumping site. A sudden shadow caused Twitch to look up, and the rusty, pockmarked sides of the huge Dumpship obscured the blinding, sweltering light of Plato. At last, she had a brief respite from the toxic rays and their overwhelming smell of sulfur.

Twitch hid her Cycler in an old, dented bronze cabinet to prevent other Scavengers from finding and stealing it. It was much too heavy and cumbersome to lug back and forth between planets.

The huge bulk of the Dumpship loomed over her. Twitch took cover as the ship's underbelly opened and the latest load of refuse from the Londonsphere tumbled with deafening clangs and crashes to the piles below. Once the hailstorm of garbage ceased, Twitch darted out of her hiding place and waited until the underside of the ship closed, and the Dumpship fired its engines in preparation to leave the moon's atmosphere.

At the last second, she shot a grappling hook up and over the gondola railing and clambered up, her sacks clipped to a harness on her back. The grappling hook gun was one of her most precious purchases.

Twitch hunkered down behind some coils of rope and waited. Once the Dumpship left the moon's atmosphere, guards would be patrolling, looking for any creature doing exactly what Twitch was doing now. She would have to be nimble and quick to evade them during the trip.

An hour later, the Dumpship reentered the Londonsphere's dome and docked. Twitch crept out from behind an empty crate and made a dash for the hatch. As she darted through the ship's exit, a guard spotted her and shouted something, but Twitch ignored him and raced off, lugging her two heavy sacks behind her. She slipped through the gate at the entrance of the Dumpship Docking Zone.

Weaving in and out of dark, dingy alleyways, Twitch finally stopped, clutching a stitch in her side. She had arrived in front of a shabby building with a creaking sign above the door.

The building had strips of peeling black paint clinging to weathered boards, and a breeze whistled around its five rusted chimneys, giving the place an air of menace. The sign said

Barker's Elicit Emporium and Pawnbrokers.

Below that hung another notice.

Auction Nights Once a Mooncycle.

And below that was another notice.

Closed.

Twitch ignored the last sign and pushed open the door. It was dark inside Barker's, save for a few greasy oil lamps casting weird shadows on the walls. She hurried across the dimly lit space to a dingy counter. There were years' worth of carvings embedded into the wood, and oil stains covering its surface. Twitch rang the hand bell and began pulling items from her first, lining them up on the counter. After a moment, an old angry dwarf dressed in a filthy duster coat two sizes too big waddled out from the back room. His face lit up behind his scraggly grey beard as he spied Twitch. Or more accurately, Twitch's load of things.

No one else was inside the Emporium, save a large, hooded lizard loitering in a corner. Twitch quickly gestured to the line of items and eyed the dwarf across the counter. The dwarf peered into it and sifted through the contents.

"Five gold. For the lot," the dwarf grunted. Twitch was indignant.

"Twelve!" replied Twitch.

"Seven." The dwarf was stubborn.

"Ten." Twitch thought she could get by on ten gold for a Mooncycle. Her sister, Jadyn, worked as a performer, and Twitch had kept the tail brace for her, as well as the other sack of salvaged bits and bobs. Her sister was a mean fence if and when the need arose.

"Fine." The dwarf pushed a stack of coins across the counter.

Twitch grabbed them and hastily stuffed them into her waist pouch. She left Barker's and headed through the narrow alleys, looking for the square where the East Way Performers were set up. Jadyn would love that tail brace.

THE SPEEDING VELOCIPEDE

In a dingy house in the poorer part of the Residential district, a woman sat on a cushion, eyes closed. Another woman sat across from her, nervously clutching a small coin purse.

The woman on the cushion breathed in and out slowly, the black beads on her ragged shawl glittering slightly in the lamplight as she let the familiar feeling of fading take hold of her. The gift of Shadowsight was a highly prized and rare talent, and normally anyone who showed signs of having it would be sent down to the Motherworld to work for the Dualworld Society.

But not the Seer. She had hidden her talents from the Constabulary Droids. She had no wish to leave the world in which she had been born to go and work for a group of nutters on the Surface who were obsessed with the Dualworld and wanted ... what? No one outside the society knew what they were up to and frankly, she didn't want to know.

The feeling of fading grew stronger, and was accompanied by a tugging sensation. The Seer let the tug carry her down, left, right, up slightly, and finally she came to rest. She opened her eyes slowly and peered around. Wisps of black fog drifted lazily through the air, and more came off the shadowy furnishings of her parlor.

She peered through the haze, seeing the dark shadowy form of the woman's Dual sitting across from her. Behind the woman stood a man, clad in faded grey garments that looked to be the rough attire of a Sifter. He lifted his blank face to meet the Seer's gaze and raised an arm, writing in the air with a spectral finger. Black words appeared, and the Seer slowly read them aloud.

Clementine Ives watched fearfully as the figure of the Seer wobbled like a mirage. The Seer's eyes opened, and Clementine squeaked in horror when she saw that they were a shimmering, oily black, with little tendrils of black mist escaping at the edges. The Seer opened her mouth, and in a flat monotone began to recite the poem that Clementine's dear dead Alfred had written for her. Clementine began to shake. And cry. And wish she had never come. This was too much.

A year ago, Clem's dear husband Alfred had been hauled off by the Constabulary Ship. For what, she could not begin to guess. A year without her dear Alfred had been the hardest thing she had ever endured, and at last in a fit of weakness, Clem had seized her coin purse, filled it with all her savings, and gone to seek out the Seer.

The Seer finished up the poem and nodded to the smoky apparition. He nodded back and started to withdraw. The Seer pulled herself farther out of her body and stood up, now fully in the Dualworld. She stretched and yawned and wandered about the room for a minute before sighing and settling back onto her cushion. It was so nice to get out and about. She really ought to do it more often. She closed her eyes and gave her consciousness a sharp yank.

Later that night, Clementine Ives, now two crowns poorer, tripped while walking home and was run down by a speeding velocipede.

Meanwhile, back in her hovel, the Seer bit into a lovely juicy fruit and chewed contentedly. What a fruitful night it had been.

Rich Pickings

Belladonna hugged her ragged wool cloak tighter around her shoulders and waited, poised in a doorway across from the street performers.

A tattered flag with faded loopy lettering was stuck in a barrel next to them, proclaiming them to be *The East Way Performers*. She watched as a Cat in a hood and aviation goggles pulled a Cat dancer aside for a moment. Belladonna caught a glimpse of bronze gears as the first Cat clicked a mechanical tail brace onto the other Cat's tail. Then, the second Cat rejoined the dance.

Belladonna picked at an old, unsloughed scale on her arm as she waited for them to finish their routine. Her hood was pulled low over her eyes, shielding her smooth, thick, tentacle dreadlocks from view. As the performers finished their routine and passersby tossed a motley collection of little bronze coins into a beaten top hat, Belladonna made her move.

Swiftly, she probed the air in front of her with a finger, until she detected a slight tug in the Aether. She reached her largest tentacle out of her hood, and ejected the barb at the end, piercing the air where she felt the pull. The air around her rippled outwards, and as the ripple reached the performers and the crowd, they all froze in place. Quickly, Belladonna scuttled through the immobilized crowd to the top hat. She was just scooping the coins into a small bag at her waist when she saw a fat silver coin suspended in the air, having just left the fingers of a fellow dressed in slightly finer clothes than those around him.

Belladonna dithered for a moment, pondering whether to break the spell by interacting with those frozen to seize the coin. After a moment's hesitation, Belladonna retracted her tentacle barb and snatched the coin, breaking the spell on the crowd. By the time the group noticed the disappearance of the hat and their money, Belladonna was already ducking into a nearby alley out of sight.

A week later, Belladonna was standing in the same doorway, dressed in a smart, new, dark-green hood and brown leather trousers. She lifted her head, the delicate pattern of scales on her cheekbones shimmering ever so slightly in the light of the oil lamp suspended above her in the doorway arch. Her large, luminescent eyes gleamed as she saw the money hat, a bowler this time, laid out in plain view, already nearly brimming with coins. Rich pickings today.

Belladonna eyed up the crowd. They all seemed fairly new to this performance, hopefully so new that they wouldn't recognize her if the spell went wrong. Quickly, the Cogling probed the air in front of her once again.

At this moment, one of the performers leapt out of the dance routine and snatched the bowler off the ground. He was a Wolverine, clad in trousers and a woolen hood, not unlike Belladonna's own attire.

He hissed, and the crowd scattered. The other performers grabbed the flag off its stand and the Wolverine beckoned them around. Each opened a waist pouch, and the wolverine divvied up the money equally. Then he popped the bowler onto his head and the group melted away, weaving into alleyways like dirty water filtering into the cracks between cobblestones.

Belladonna scowled and did the same. A tipoff about a dwarf interested her greatly. She slid off into the darkness, in search of Barker's Elicit Emporium and Pawnbrokers.

THE EAST WAY PERFORMERS

Waverly executed a double turn, eyeing the hooded figure in the doorway with suspicion. It had been there every day for the past week, and every day for the past week the troupe's earnings had mysteriously vanished. Odd indeed.

He lifted Jadyn in a triple aerial spin. The nimble Cat twirled above him, and Waverly noticed that Jadyn's head was turned in the same direction as his. Her sister, Twitch, had stopped by to give her an impeccably made tail brace. Waverly was thrilled, devising new routines in his head that would make the most of Jadyn's new acquisition.

As he lowered her, she hissed, "You were right. They are here again. Initiate our plan after the next sequence."

Waverly, desperate to rescue their livelihood from such blatant thievery, had devised a plan to protect it with the rest of the East Way Performers. Now he watched the suspicious figure reach out and stroke the air in front of them, and he knew they were about to steal the most money the troupe had earned in their career.

The large wolverine spun, dipped Phantom the ferret, and then leapt into action. He seized his bowler hat and snarled menacingly, causing the crowd to scatter. He snatched the troupe's banner as Jadyn and a Greater Spryte named Tempest quickly folded the faded red cloth into a square and tucked it away in some hidden pocket.

Waverly quickly divvied up the money into the team's belt pouches, then signaled for them to disperse and meet back at their lodgings. The figure in the shadows did not make a move, and as Waverly rushed by, he thought he caught a glimpse of shimmery scales and the glint of a luminous eye.

Later that evening, Waverly flipped through a large leatherbound volume entitled, *"Zaleria Von Stein's Account of Most Known Species."* He stopped on a page with a detailed drawing of a Western Manticore, then moved on.

Jadyn appeared at his side bearing a bowl of hot soup, and sat with him for a while, talking about this, that, and the other thing. Waverly briefly paid attention when she mentioned a theatre called *"Moira and Grace's Theatric Co.,"* and how they might be able to book a spot there. And when she nodded off against his shoulder, Waverly let her stay there while he flipped endlessly through his book. He just had to know *what* the hooded figure had been, if not who.

With the gas lamp at his side dimming, Waverly let the book drop from his aching paws. He gently shifted Jadyn onto his bed and pulled the quilt over her. Then he got up and walked over to her hammock. His foot kicked *"Zaleria Von Stein's Account of Most Known Species"* and it flipped over on the floor, into that position that careless creatures leave their volumes, where gravity slowly cracks the spine.

Waverly picked it up huffily, and as he did so, the pages fell open on *Cogling*. It read,

"A rare but powerful breed. These highly intelligent creatures are originally from the planet Zorah-7, which was consumed by a dying star. Though some Coglings

are thought to have escaped, they are now numbered and

far between, scattered across the universe."

Waverly eyed the picture triumphantly. At last. The Cogling stared back at him from the page, her large opalescent eyes gleaming at him mischievously. Her head full of long, thick tentacles was covered in a pattern of delicate pointed scales.

Waverly marked the page, climbed into Jadyn's hammock, and closed his eyes. The money had been saved, and a Cogling thief outsmarted. And their troupe could possibly get a booking in a real theatre! That would be an adventure. But then, adventures are common in a city so fraught with creatures and their disagreements.

Launch When Ready

Odessa stared out the window at the hazy rooftops below, watching a dark speck scale a drainpipe. The speck made it about halfway up when a glint of silver heralded the arrival of a dagger, flying through the air. The speck tumbled down out of her line of sight. Odessa sighed.

She checked the enormous clock on the wall next to her and sighed again. The black mahogany sides contained whirring gears and tumblers, and it was wound to exactly match the times shown on the clocks down on the Motherworld. It was nearly time to send out a signal to the Reception Bay and let the workers know to get the Londonsphere's ration-import ready.

The large Black Tufted Squirrel gave one last withering look at the skyscape and turned, pressing down on a polished wooden lever set into the wall. Out rumbled a tangle of black metal tubes and churning cogs. Odessa flicked a few switches and unhooked the mouthpiece.

"Hello?" she said. "This is the Londonsphere. Overseer Odessa speaking. We are prepared to eject our Citadel Pod and pick up our next load of rations."

There was a crackle of static and a voice spoke. "Your message has been received. Cargo ready for pickup this time next Suncycle. Please hold."

Odessa scuttled down the iron spiral stairs that led from the Observation Tower into the bowels of the Citadel. She passed other Overseers, all similarly dressed in black breeches, black tunics, and black velvet cloaks. Odessa strode purposefully through the passages, making her way steadily to the Notary Machine.

The Notary Machine was a huge contraption much like the machine she used to speak with the Motherworld. It amplified and carried her voice to loudspeakers throughout the Citadel. It was used to inform the rest of the Overseers about trips to the Motherworld, to call in the Overseers' Cavalry to deal with large problems in the Londonsphere, or for emergencies and critical announcements.

Odessa flicked a switch, and a large wooden lever ejected from the machine's side. The Squirrel bore down on the lever with all her strength, and when it clicked into place, she took down the mouthpiece. She was now broadcasting.

"Attention Citadel," she said, hearing her own voice, magnified and distorted, echoing through the black marble halls. "At one full Suncycle we will eject down to the Motherworld. There, rations and supplies will be loaded into the Factory for inventory and dispersed to all Londonsphere merchants. This is a routine drill. No special requirements will be needed. Thank you."

Odessa hung the mouthpiece back on its hook and shoved the lever up again, cutting off the broadcast. She flipped the switch, sliding the lever back into its compartment, and closed the door to the Notary Room as she left.

Later that evening, Odessa lay on her bunk set high in the wall and looked at the small photo of her sister, framed in black. Kandyl worked as a tinker on the Motherworld. When Odessa was chosen to become an Overseer on the Londonsphere, the sisters had said a tearful farewell in the front room of their father's

Smithery. A year later, the Cloven sisters' parents were dead, and Kandyl had taken over the business.

Odessa sighed and turned the knob next to her bunk to switch off the gaslight. She pulled the black blanket up to her chin.

The next morning, Odessa woke early. She dressed in her tunic and breeches, pulled her velvet cloak over her head, and hurried to the Observation tower, which doubled as the Ejection Booth.

Sure enough, the Motherworld had sent a command up to the tower, causing a switchboard to slide out of a panel in the wall. She would use this to operate the Citadel Ejection Mechanism, and shoot the entire Citadel through a tube of electromagnetic energy in space, down to the Motherworld to collect supplies for the entire Londonsphere.

Odessa grabbed the mouthpiece for the communicator and spoke into it. "This is the Londonsphere," she said, "ready to launch on your command. Overseer Odessa piloting."

A voice replied, "Overseer Odessa, this is Loading Volunteer Kandyl. Launch when ready."

Odessa was speechless. "Kandyl?" she said.

"Launch when ready, Overseer Odessa," Kandyl's voice came again.

Odessa collected herself. She flicked some switches and pulled a lever. Then, she pressed a foot pedal. The Great Gear Wall surrounding the Citadel began to churn. The Citadel began to sink slowly through a massive metal tube in the ground. Through the Observation Tower windows, Odessa watched the ground slowly rise. As the top of the Citadel sank beneath ground level, Odessa took a deep breath.

If she pushed the electromagnetic pulser button too soon, the entire Londonsphere could be engulfed in a wave of electricity strong enough to kill the entire population. Too late, and the Citadel would not latch onto the tube of opposing energy and could be hurled into the eye of the nebula. All within would perish. Not her favorite part of piloting duty.

Through narrowed eyes, Odessa watched as the sections of pipe raced by, faster and faster. Every ounce of her focus was on the task at hand, and her entire body was taut with concentration. Then, at the exact right moment, just as the Citadel exited the pipe, she pushed the button. The entire cluster of buildings shot out of the bottom of the Londonsphere, its dome containing the oxygen within. The electromagnetic pulses locked and held, and the Citadel was sent down a straight course for the Motherworld.

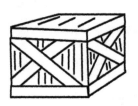

A Tiny Dot of Light

Kandyl stood in a massive bronze dome.

In the overwrought style of the Motherworld, the Receiving Bay for the Londonsphere had a retractable roof that allowed the Citadel Pod to dock and pick up food and supplies for the population of their moon.

The Grey Tufted Squirrel was wearing the brown leather overalls of a worker, and she had her tinker goggles pushed up on her forehead. She stood, her tail vibrating in suppressed excitement. Her sister Odessa worked as an Overseer on the Londonsphere, keeping the surplus population that had been moved there from the Motherworld calm and happy. The last time Kandyl had seen Odessa was when her sister had left for the Londonsphere a year ago, before their parents had died, leaving Kandyl in charge of the family tinker business.

Kandyl looked up. A tiny dot of light was growing bigger by the moment. It was speeding down toward the Receiving Bay, and Odessa was piloting. Kandyl backed up slightly as the Citadel touched down in a hiss of steam. She pressed herself against the stacks of crates and sacks as the enormous building settled into its dock, sending clouds of hot water vapor into the air, carrying the scent of oil. A horde of other workers began seizing boxes and barrels and carrying them over to the Citadel's massive cargo hold entrance.

The front doors of the Citadel opened and a sea of creatures in black velvet cloaks streamed out. Some Overseers began directing the workers and telling them what was most needed. Some

Overseers left the Receiving Bay entirely and went to speak to the Record Keeper to relay recent events, or to speak with the Motherworld Council about passing new laws. Others delivered particularly devious criminals who could not be contained safely on the Londonsphere. A prison wagon trundled out of the Citadel's front doors, packed to bursting with creatures of all sorts. Another wagon followed the first, but these creatures were blessed with the gift of Shadowsight, and were destined to join the Dualworld Society where they would hone their abilities and be initiated into the group of supernatural scientists.

Kandyl stood and surveyed the sea of Overseers, trying to pick out a black fluffy tail and long tufted ears from the crowd. At last she spotted Odessa, standing near the Citadel wall. She rushed toward her sister, pushing her way through the throng.

"Odessa! Odessa!" she called. At last, she reached her. Odessa whirled around, her face breaking into a smile.

"Kandyl! What are you doing here?" she asked. "I didn't know you're a Receiving Bay worker."

"I'm not," Kandyl laughed. "I'm volunteering. I hoped I would see you here."

Odessa wrapped Kandyl in a hug, her black cloak enveloping them both.

"It's so good to see you, Kandie," Odessa whispered. "Any news? How is … everything?"

Kandyl hugged her tighter. "You too, Odie. It's good to see you, too. We have so much to catch up on. The Uprising … it has begun."

EPILOGUE

This galaxy has stars, and asteroids, and glowy nebulas, just like any other galaxy. It has planets and moons—and inhabitants that don't always get on with each other.

This being-made planet is surrounded by smaller planetoids of metal and rock, some orbiting the planet like sickly moons, and some attached to it with chains and harpoons. The moons of organic material provide the metal planet with grains and other foods, and the other moons are dumping grounds for surplus population and the general waste of the planet.

The surplus population have their own little societies, and they name their moons after great cities throughout the universe, heard about through the stories of travelers.

This particular planet is filled with magic. This particular planet has adventures like no other.

Acknowledgements

First and foremost, I would like to thank my mentor, Nicholas, for bolstering my stories and my skills to new heights.

I would like to thank my teacher, Mrs. Anderson, for keeping this part of the eighth grade experience alive through such a difficult year.

I would like to thank my mom, for believing in me, and for that epic final proofread!

And I would like to thank my cat, Olive, for sitting on my computer at all the wrong times. You wore out the backspace button my friend!

Oh, and one last thing. I want to thank all the people reading this right now. That means you've made it this far in my book, and you actually care enough to read the acknowledgements! (Or you're one of the people mentioned before, and you're just reading my compliments).

Thank you all so much!

—NORA